COLOUR JETS

# UNDER THE RED ELEPHANT

Jan Mark and Jeffrey Reid

Collins

# COLOUR JETS

First published in Great Britain
by HarperCollins*Publishers* Ltd 1995

The HarperCollins website address is
www.**fire**and**water**.com

12 11 10 9 8 7 6 5 4

Text © Jan Mark 1995
Illustrations © Jeffrey Reid 1995

The author and illustrator assert the moral right to be
identified as the author and illustrator of the work.

A CIP record for this title is available
from the British Library.

ISBN 0 00 675032 X

Printed in Hong Kong

# Chapter 1

It is an Australian elephant.

"No such thing," says Kade, when I tell him.

Elephants come from Africa and India.

"And Burma," says Brett, who knows everything.

"But not Australia," Kade says.

Unless it's a sort of kangaphant that hops through the bush with its baby in a bag.

"A pouch," said Brett.
"Or a koalaphant, that lives in
a tree," said Kade.
"Or a budgeriphant," added Brett.

I say, "It comes from Australia and it's an elephant."

Gran brought it back when she went to see Aunt Emma.

Or an Emmaphant.

How did she get it home?

In a jumbo jet. Boom-boom!

Who needs enemies with friends like them?

My real enemy is called Robert Friend.

This makes life very difficult.

The elephant is red and rubbery, and when it comes out of its box it looks like an elephant skin that shrank in the wash.

"Seems a bit dead," says Dad.
"Let's give it some air."

The elephant skin has a nozzle
at the end of its trunk.
Dad blows into it.

And blows.

And blows.

The elephant skin
begins to move about
in a nasty way.

Now it looks like an
elephant that has been
stomped on by a herd
of other elephants who
didn't like it much.

Dad has the loudest voice in our street. He is known as "Leather-lungs". But even with leather lungs, Dad can't do much with the elephant. The skin is too thick.

censored!

Now it looks like an elephant with a horrible disease. Nicky sees it and starts to cry.

Get the foot pump.

You get the foot pump, Brains.

The foot pump is very slow. Mum, Dad and I take turns, and the elephant flops about as if it is dying in agony.

The elephant swells and swells.
Nicky screams and screams.
Mum says she will have nightmares and takes her away.

Then the elephant shoots off the foot pump, whizzes across the room, jams itself under the television and lies there getting smaller and smaller and making a noise like a million raspberries as the air comes out.

"You know what?" says Dad. "I think this is a bad idea."

"Well, I've got a good idea," says Mum, coming back.

12

We'll take it to the fete on Saturday and get it filled with helium.

I know about helium. It is the lightest thing in the universe. When you see jokes about people being swept away over the roof tops by a bunch of balloons, that is what is in the balloons –

helium.

13

## Chapter 2

Now, if I were arranging our trip to the fete it would be me and Kade and Brett, with a lot of money and no grown-ups.

But I am not arranging it. Mum is. Kade and Brett are going on their own with no grown-ups and not much money.

I am going with Mum and Nicky, which is all right if you can't get out of it.

Also, we are taking my dim cousins, Julie and Justin, which is not all right, but I can't get out of that, either.

Dad is working on Saturday, which is very sensible of him.

15

On Saturday, after lunch, we are ready to go. Me, Mum, Julie, Justin and Nicky in the buggy, and one dead elephant in a string bag. Mum hangs the bag behind the buggy so Nicky can't see it.

The fete is in Victoria Park. There is a banner over the gate saying FETE, in case you do not know what a fete looks like.

FETE

There's also a big sign with a list of all the things that are happening inside, in case you are too stupid to notice the funfair, the donkey rides, the Punch and Judy and the band stand.

FETE
FUNFAIR
PUNCH + JUDY
SPLAT THE TEACHER!
BANDS
DONKEY RIDES

LOTS OF FUN !

There are three bands playing.

The brass band…

… the silver band…

… and the steel band, which is my favourite.

There ought to be an elastic band too!

This is the oldest joke in the world. I ought to know. I made it up last year.

I say, "Can I go and find Kade and Brett? We promised to meet each other at the donkey rides."

Mum says, "No one is going anywhere until we get the elephant up. Stay here."

Over by the fence a man is selling balloons. He has a tank of helium for blowing them up. A lot of people have already bought balloons, and already a lot of them are stuck in trees or sailing away towards Birmingham.

Come down.

Mum takes the string bag and goes over to Helium-man. They have a long chat about how many balloons worth of helium it will take to fill an elephant.

Money changes hands.

Mum takes out the elephant skin and I turn the buggy round so that Nicky won't see what is happening.

The elephant is
coming to life.
It lifts its trunk,
its tail waves,
its legs kick,
its ears flap.

At last it looks like
a real elephant.

Mum comes back and the elephant is sailing over her head on a long string.

She shows it to Nicky.

"Toilet," says Nicky,
but she does not scream.

She does not know
that the lovely elephant
is the horrible, wobbly
red thing that flopped
about on the floor.

Look Nicky!
Lovely elephant.

!

Mum ties the string to the
handle of the buggy.

"Now," she says, "this is our
flag. This is where we are.
If anyone gets lost, just
look for the red elephant."

TOILET
NOW!

I want
some
candyfloss!

I want to
see Punch
and Judy!

I want to find Kade
and Brett but I don't
say so. Babies and
dim people have
to be seen to first.

27

## Chapter 3

Mum takes Nicky to the Ladies, which is a sort of caravan.

Justin, Julie and I stand by the buggy.
People admire our elephant.
Then the worst happens.
Guess who comes round the
corner of the fortune-teller's tent...?

It is my deadly enemy,
Robert Friend.

"Stupid elephant," says Robert Friend.

If that string broke, or somebody cut it, that elephant would fly up over the trees and interfere with air traffic.

They'd have to call out the army and shoot it down.

"Fancy coming out with a lot of little kids,"
says Robert Friend.
"Fancy coming out with
your mummy-wummy."

My mummy-wummy
comes back from the
Ladies with Nicky.
She is twice as tall
as Robert Friend.

Robert Friend
melts into the
crowd.

"Who else wants to see the
Punch and Judy?" says Mum.
No one does.
"Who else wants candyfloss?"
We all do.
"Right," says Mum. "Candyfloss all
round while I take Justin to see the
Punch and Judy."
We cannot take Nicky to the Punch
and Judy because it makes her scream.
I don't know why.

Mr Punch doesn't
do anything that
Nicky doesn't do,
like bashing people
over the head,
for instance.

33

"Now," says Mum, "go where you like, but stay together. We won't be long."

"Suppose we get lost," says dim Julie. "Suppose you can't find us again?"

I shall know where to find you shan't I? Under the red elephant!

Off she goes, with Justin.

Julie and Nicky and I walk about,
under the red elephant.

We watch people throwing wet sponges
at teachers, for charity, and a man
sitting in a bath full of baked
beans, for charity, and three boys
fighting because they feel like it.

## Chapter 4

Nicky is turning as red as the elephant.
She definitely wants to go now.

If Julie weren't so dim she would think
of a joke about this. But she just says,
"Oh, all right then."

Julie takes Nicky into the Ladies. There must be a queue. They are gone a long time.

Then up come Kade and Brett.

Where have you been? We waited and waited by the donkeys.

Then we saw your Kangaphant.

So we knew you must be under it.

Kade and Brett have brought ice lollies,
so we sit down and eat them.

Or we start to. Suddenly Brett says,
"Oi! Get off! Come here!
Come back!"
And jumps up.
Kade jumps up.

I look round.

Robert Friend
has hi-jacked
our elephant!

41

## Chapter 5

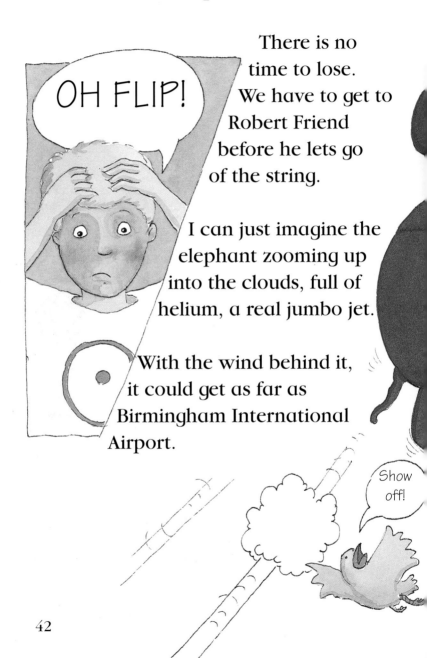

OH FLIP!

There is no time to lose. We have to get to Robert Friend before he lets go of the string.

I can just imagine the elephant zooming up into the clouds, full of helium, a real jumbo jet.

With the wind behind it, it could get as far as Birmingham International Airport.

Show off!

It might get mixed up with other jumbos.

Air Traffic Control will see an alien blob on the radar screens.

People will report UFOs.

Missiles will be launched. World War III will be started by an elephant!

Very Big Bomb

I forget about dim Julie and Nicky. I run after Brett and Kade who are running after our enemy, Robert Friend, and the red elephant.

For some reason I do not forget the buggy, but this turns out to be a good thing. People get out of our way when they see us coming. Brett, Kade, me and the buggy.

45

The air is full of floating things.

There are balloons on strings, and balloons that have escaped, and balloons with labels that are racing.

A lot of people have had the same idea that we did.

One family
has a banana
on a pole to
show where
they are.

One has a
green
caterpillar.

Another has a
gorilla.

But no one
else has a red
elephant.

47

Kade and Brett and me and the buggy race between tents and under guy ropes and over picnics, while the elephant flies along in front of us.

Oops!

We go twice round the fete, I think, and then run into Mum and Justin, heading the same way.

Then she stops.

She remembers.

"But *you've* got the elephant," she says.

Then she sees the empty buggy.

Just then we see dim Julie belting along,
dragging Nicky. Nicky is sort of
scraping along the grass because she
can't keep up.

There
they are!

"Julie, come back!"
Mum yells, and
goes after them.

And then Brett says, "It's gone."

Ian went off and left us chasing the elephant.

But I'm here aren't I? I haven't got the elephant.

We all look round.

The elephant has vanished.

I don't see it.

If he's burst it I'll…

We cheer ourselves up by thinking what Mum will do when she catches our enemy, Robert Friend.

53

We find Robert Friend near the donkey rides. With him are his brothers, Bill and Eric Friend.

Mrs Friend is there too, with a carrier full of greasy burgers.

Robert, I believe you have our elephant.

I never.

"I don't see any elephants," says Bill.

"Last elephant I saw was ten feet tall. Kind of hard to miss," adds Eric.

55

And then Nicky points and starts to
scream. The pile of coats has begun to
move. They tremble and heave and fall
on to the rug.

SHRIEEK!

Out of the middle of the heap rises our
red elephant.

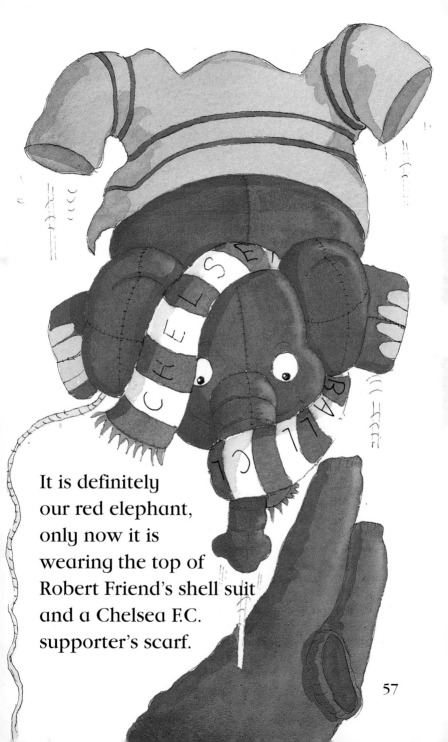

It is definitely
our red elephant,
only now it is
wearing the top of
Robert Friend's shell suit
and a Chelsea F.C.
supporter's scarf.

Kade and Brett and me
all make a dive for the string.

Mrs Friend drops the bag
of burgers.

No one catches the string.

59

We all sit there watching the elephant heading for outer space. It doesn't go up like an ordinary balloon, it moves at elephant speed, very dignified.

Well, that's the last we've seen of that!

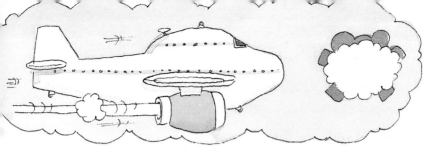

Just as I am thinking that it really will
go to Birmingham International, it
comes up against the branch of a tree.
It hangs there underneath it, like a big
Red Delicious elephant.

Never mind our elephant!

So Bill and Eric have to climb the tree. Robert and lots of their friends gather round and jump up and down, chanting.

FALL! FALL! FALL!

But they don't fall. They reach the
elephant and tie
the string to the
lace of Eric's
left boot.

Very slowly
the elephant
comes back
down again,
like a paratrooper.

So Robert Friend gets his shell suit back
and Bill and Eric are stuck up the tree
and Mrs Friend is stuck in the burgers.

Me and Mum and Nicky, and dim Julie and Justin, and Kade and Brett and the elephant, all go and have some more candyfloss.

And some of us are sick on the way home.